Maggie Matheson
Short and Sweet

CW01551187

ISBN: 9798314450079

This book is dedicated to our mum, Gladys

There is a lot of Mum in Maggie. Mum wasn't a spy (as far as I know!) but she did enjoy life and she had a great sense of humour, just like Maggie.

I like to think that she lives on in Britain's favourite octogenarian spy.

Contents

Maggie Matheson: Short and Sweet

Chapter 1

Maggie sat on a lounger in the far corner of the balcony, huddled up against the wall. It was the only place outside that gave shelter from the brisk southeasterly, currently whipping across the Adelaide beach below her. She had a tartan blanket wrapped around her red cardigan-clad shoulders, thick black tights under her tartan skirt, and a tartan thermos on the small glass coffee table next to her.

She was all too aware of 'The Clash of the Tartans' – second husband Dingo's take on Maggie's current choice of attire and accoutrements – but to be honest, with no Scottish blood and no loyalty to any clan, she didn't give a 'haggis's arse' (as Dingo, might say) what tartan she sported. She was warm and that was the main thing. Something she wasn't expecting not to be when she agreed that she and Dingo would live half the year in Australia and half in the UK.

They had opted to spend their northern hemisphere summers wintering in the southern hemisphere and their southern hemisphere summers wintering in the northern hemisphere. When Dingo had presented it to her like that, her brain – sharp as a pin in her spying heyday – had struggled to grasp what winters were summered in which hemisphere. Though well-travelled in her career as a spy, she had always struggled with time zones. Add to that the change in seasons – and Dingo's propensity to lack clarity at times – and she was left bamboozled.

'I couldn'ta explained it easier, Maggs,' an exasperated Dingo had said. 'If it helps, think of it the other way: would you rather be spending your northern hemisphere winters summering in the southern hemisphere and your southern hemisphere winters summering in the northern hemisphere… or not?'

'Not what?'

'Not spending your northern hemisphere winters summering in the southern hemisphere and your southern hemisphere winters summering in the northern hemisphere.'

In the end, she had sat in a dark corner, closed her eyes and walked through the concept in her mind. She pictured herself getting on a plane at Heathrow Airport in July, wearing sandals, a chiffon dress and sunglasses, and getting off at Brisbane Airport wearing the same thing, then imagining telling her friends at the Frampton Bridge Club when she got back to the UK how amazing it was to be wearing summer clothes, *even though it's the middle of their winter there!* Then she imagined the same journey in reverse in January in the same attire; sweltering getting on the plane in the glare of the summer sun in Brisbane and arriving in London, trying to see anything through sunglasses with the low, bleak, grey skies overhead, and having to cope with the frozen steps down to the tarmac in sandals, the icy wind blowing her chiffon dress all over the place.

When put like that, it didn't sound that attractive.

In practice, though, the arrangement worked: Maggie struggled in the extreme heat of Australian and even British summers at times. Dingo didn't. But being Dingo, he was happy to go along with whatever Maggie wanted which was to spend autumn and winter in the UK over Christmas, and autumn and winter in Oz when it was nicely warm, not too hot. And they mitigated the effects of the weather extremes by leaving the UK in March and returning in September. They would soon be returning to the UK after this visit to Adelaide from their usual base in Brisbane to see Dingo's daughter, Flo.

It was chilly now, though, at nine o'clock on a late September, South Australian Spring morning. Dingo opened the sliding doors from the modest, but comfortable, two-bedroomed apartment they were renting in Glenelg, enough for him to poke his head through.

'Why doncha come inside for your breakfast, Maggs?' he pleaded. 'You must be freezing your nuts off.'

'If I had any nuts – and be clear that I would have told you before we got married if I did – they would be nice and snug underneath the precautions I have taken to keep them, and the rest of me, nice and snug.'

'Your nose is blue. Come inside. I've got some eggs on the go.'

'It's sunny. I'm British. If the sun is out, we British have to sit in it. Even if it's cold enough to freeze the nuts of those unlucky enough to possess them.'

'It's nine degrees, Maggs.'

'I'm toasty, thank you, which is how I'd like the things my eggs are presented to me on to be, please, preferably with a plate and a tray underneath too. Don't bother about the tea.' She tapped her thermos. 'I've still plenty in here.'

'Maggs, come on in, you soppy galah.'

'Stop fussing, I'm fine.'

She had been tempted to reinforce her fineness with a wag of the finger in Dingo's direction, but it would have meant taking one of them away from under her warm armpits. Besides, she had been trying to stop the finger-wagging, ever since Flo had pointed out that she kept doing it. A lot.

It had bothered Maggie. She never used to be a finger-wagger. In her youth, she had always found ways to get across her point well enough without it, usually through her choice of words, or in extreme situations, through the wagging of a Browning automatic revolver. The ironic thing was that not only was the finger she raised and wagged her trigger finger, but it was also slightly crooked as if she were about to pull that trigger.

'You put your head down slightly too when you do it,' Flo had told her. 'You nod knowledgeably, your finger goes up in front of you, and you crook your finger as you make your point.'

'I do not, young lady!' Maggie had insisted, nodding knowledgeably with her head down slightly, her crooked finger wagging away in front of her.

From then on, she had done her best to make sure her finger was missing in action when she spoke to people. It was a habit she was keen to break. After all, it wasn't even as if the points she was making were that important to warrant any sort of hand gesture to reinforce them. *You're British Maggs,* she reminded herself. *Not Italian.*

Ah, the Italians… her favourite country and people. She remembered well that British Secret Service case, a few years ago, when she had gone undercover as an Italian nonna, the mother of the leader of a cybergang. Perhaps that propensity to wear her heart on her sleeve and show how she felt, like many Italians, was one of the reasons it had been successful.

The case had been one of many fond – and not so fond – memories she had of her time in the Service. The role, and the opportunity to reconcile with Bill, her long-lost son, had tempted her out of retirement at the age of eighty. That was all behind her now. She was definitely retired now: tired, retired and re-retired. At eighty-four, she was much more comfortable putting *criminals* down as the answer to a crossword clue (six down, one word, 9 letters in this month's *The Lady* Cryptic) than putting up with the cross words from criminals she'd help put away. Yes, she enjoyed the life of a retiree – even when she was outside sitting on a balcony in Adelaide, freezing her nuts off.

The doors opened again and Dingo squeezed through, holding a tray with two fried eggs on two pieces of brown toast, a glass of freshly squeezed orange juice and a steaming mug of freshly ground coffee for him. When they first arrived, he had been thrilled to see the apartment was well-equipped with mod cons. He was less thrilled when he found out he required a degree in computer science to use half of them.

'Why do I need a bloody app to use the TV?' he had moaned at Maggie, who for once was in full agreement with her partner. 'And I'm gonna need to order a magnifying glass off the internet to read the bloody wi-fi code on the back of the router. Oh, wait… I can't get online to order the blasted thing coz I can't see the blasted wi-fi code.'

'You could take a picture of the code and zoom in.' Which is what they did… after Dingo had found his phone, another problem they regularly encountered.

'It's because we don't have our noses superglued to them like youngsters,' Maggie had complained to her daughter, Sharon. So, Sharon had shown them – several times – how to use the *Find My Device* feature on their phones. But since their phone loss normally occurred in pairs, it was useless. And even if they had one of their phones, they would forget what Sharon had shown them. They needed some sort of *Find My Find Device* guide, preferably in the form of Sharon, to find the *Find My Device* feature. On one occasion when both phones were lost, Maggie almost suggested phoning her to ask for help before she realised how tricky that would be without a phone.

'They're only called mod cons,' Dingo had claimed vociferously, 'coz they con you into thinking you can use the buggering buggers. Bloody apps and mobiles. They need to invent a phone for Luddites.'

'They already have, Dingo love. We used to have one in our hall. You could even speak into it to real people and hear what they said in response.'

The coffee machine, thankfully, did not require an app to use it. It was the same model Dingo had in his kitchen before he had sold his place in the Outback to move him and Maggie into a condo in Brisbane. He took a satisfying slurp of his coffee now as he pulled up a chair and joined Maggie near the wall.

Maggie smiled at her 'hunky outbacker'. 'Exactly how dinkum is your coffee, mate?'

'Arh, I'd say fair dinkum, thanks, Maggs. How dinkum are your googies?'

'If you mean my eggs, I want to say nicely dinkum – not over-dinkummed – thank you very much, but I'm not sure that works as Aussie slang, does it?'

Dingo chortled. 'I guess not. But I'll make an Aussie Sheila out of you yet.'

There were so many things Maggie was tempted to say in response to that, but she concentrated instead on cutting the soldier off a slice of toast and dipping it into an egg.

'Here…' Dingo placed that morning's edition of the Adelaide Herald on the coffee table. 'Cop a loada this. I found a thing called a shop that sold one of these. It's made of paper and has pictures and words on it that don't disappear when you press something you shouldn't. Wanna take a squiz at it when you've finished?'

Dingo seemed to introduce a new bit of Aussie slang every day. Truth be told, she loved it. *Squiz* could have been one of his made-up ones, though she vaguely recalled hearing it on *Neighbours* many years ago. Her mouth full of toast and egg, she nodded.

'And do you want me to catch that bit of yolk running down your chin, Maggs, or are you gonna?'

It was difficult to chew, sigh and catch the yolk with the bit of kitchen roll Dingo had thoughtfully added to the tray, but Maggie was well used to it. Was this sort of thing one of the hazards of getting old, or just a hazard of eating a perfectly runny egg?

Ever the optimist, she chose to think the latter.

Chapter 2

By the time she had finished breakfast and a mug of tea, the sun had come round and was shining onto the balcony. Dingo popped back inside to clear the plates, leaving Maggie to flip through the Adelaide Herald. She didn't flip very far because a headline on page two caught her eye:

East German Artist Claims Asylum

The headline alone raised questions. The Cold War had finished, certainly as far as East Germany was concerned, with the Berlin Wall coming down in 1989. Those days of prisoner exchanges through Checkpoint Charlie, or escapes over or under the wall were a thing of the past.

Her curiosity piqued, she read on:

Sculptor and textile artist, Oliver Steinman, 87, has put in an application to the UK government, claiming political asylum, 35 years after the German Democratic Republic (GDR) collapsed and Germany was reunified. Steinman has spent the intervening years living in isolation on a farm in a remote area, ten miles outside Berlin.

Two weeks before the wall came down, Steinman, wanted by the GDR for selling state secrets to the West, went into hiding. Since then, he had cut himself off from all aspects of society, including family, friends, the news, and modern developments, to live a hermit-like existence in a cave within, it has recently been revealed, the boundaries of the farm owned by his uncle. When his uncle died twenty years ago, the farm was taken over by entrepreneur, Ingrid Marlese, who has run the farm at arm's length through a farming management company since then.

The article went on to explain that one of the conditions of sale to Ingrid Marlese was that fuel, food, water, sanitary products, plus two bottles of 10-year-old malt whisky per month, and specific art materials as and when requested, be delivered to a shed located 100-metres away from the cave where Steinman lived. No one was to make contact with Steinman nor reveal that anyone lived there at all. In exchange, Steinman would leave occasional pieces of art which were internationally acclaimed and sold for thousands, sometimes millions, of euros. It was a good deal for Marlese and her company who would take a substantial cut of the profits, providing no questions were asked.

But now questions were being asked. Because Steinman was, unsurprisingly after 35 years, heartily fed up with living the life as a hermit in a cave, and wanted out. The problem was that the state secrets that had encouraged him to go into hiding in the first place and stay in hiding to all intents and purposes, were still very sensitive.

Although he considered himself German through his mother's heritage, he was actually Russian by way of a Russian father and a birth certificate that said he was. Coming out of hiding had its dangers. Dangers that Maggie, having been the handler 35 years ago who helped to arrange his initially 'temporary' exile on the farm, knew about only too well.

Maggie, head down and engrossed in the article, set off in a hurry back into the apartment through the patio doors – or would have done, had the glass not been in her way. With hands, head and knees somehow making contact simultaneously, she bounced off and staggered back. Dazed, she might have been in danger of flipping backwards over the balcony edge, had she not been only five feet one these days and barely able to see over the side, let alone flip over it.

In response to the loud bang on the door, Dingo jumped up from the couch and rushed towards the patio doors to help her.

There was another loud bang. As Maggie gracefully slid to the floor, she watched her husband slide less gracefully to the floor on the other side of the glass.

Life as a spy had to be considerably less dangerous than this.

Neither was seriously hurt. And '*Patiogate*', as Maggie dubbed it – ignoring Dingo's objection that the name didn't work because doors were the problem, not gates

– had given Dingo something to do while Maggie – shaken, not concussed (her favourite kind of Martini) – pondered over the article. His job was to search for masking tape (to put a big cross on the doors to prevent further accidents) in a holiday let that had all 'mod cons' but lacked, as Dingo was eager to point out, modern conveniences. With no colander, potato smasher, salt cellar, bread knife, only two plates, one small frying pan, one cereal bowl and a chopping board the size of a ten-dollar bill, there was never going to be something as handy as masking tape lurking in virtually empty drawers.

Maggie and Dingo flew back to London straight from Adelaide a few days later. The intervening time had been spent rubbing their sore noses and doing two other main activities: a good portion trying – and failing – to download an app so they could watch TV, and an even bigger portion ignoring phone calls from the British Secret Service. (Maggie might also have spent time ignoring text messages and emails from the British Secret Service had she and Dingo not used up all the little energy they allotted to solving I.T. issues on trying to download the TV app).

Maggie had spent a significant part of her career disregarding communications from the Service. It had enabled her to do her job effectively, particularly since most communications came from people who thought they could do her job much better and wanted to tell her exactly how. Some of the ones she had latterly ignored were not from people in that category. They were from fellow spies, son Bill, and great-grandson Joshua. That made the ignoring so much harder because normally she would be delighted to talk to them. But having seen the newspaper article about Steinman, she knew what they wanted, and as much as she loved them and loved her country, she just did not want to get involved again.

Dingo had agreed. 'You're retired, Maggs. You're too old to be running around European cities swinging from the rafters of the thingamy chapel in doo-dah – you know, that place in Rome where the Pope lives – or clambering up the steps of the whatchamacallit chasing after villains.'

Maggie sympathised with Dingo's lack of ability to recall the names of people and places. Goodness knows she had had enough conversations trying to remember the name of some actress who starred in a film she couldn't remember the title of, only because she thought the actress was in another film (that she couldn't remember the title of either) with the actor whose name she was trying to remember because he was in the TV programme she couldn't remember the name of that she was trying to recommend to a friend whose name she had temporarily forgotten. But she objected to Dingo stating the fact that she was too old. She was too old, of course, and that was the reason why she was ignoring the calls, but she didn't like to be told she was.

'I'm not sure I like your tone, Dingo,' she had replied, the finger set to full wag-mode. 'For a start, I have never swung from the rafters of the thingamy chapel in the doo-dah…' – she would remember the names of both those places in the middle of the night – 'I don't even think the thingamy chapel has rafters anyway. It's a dome. And I'll be the one to judge my capabilities, not you.'

'But you're ignoring the calls. And you told me that you were too old.'

'What I do and what I say are my right, not yours.'

Dingo, being Dingo, had shrugged and left it at that, but on the long flight to the UK, Maggie could not get Steinman's case out of her mind. She may be retired, but the thing was that she knew she could help.

Exactly what secrets Steinman took into hiding were only known to three people: himself, Maggie and a member of the KGB – Andrei Volkov – who would have been compromised had all those secrets been publicly revealed. That agent had had a lot to lose because of one secret in particular.

More so since he now headed up the whole organisation.

Chapter 3

Maggie paused to take a deep breath as she made her way down the steps of the plane at Heathrow Airport. Autumn was in the air – rather, it could have been, were it not suffocated by the aircraft fumes.

This was her favourite time of the year, and she was looking forward to long walks along the beach at Frampton on a sunny day, wrapped up in her favourite blue scarf that Dingo said had been knitted by one-armed Peruvian alpaca herders using the finest Merino wool in the Himalayas. Apart from being blue, it wasn't any of those things. It was cotton, machine-made and from Marks and Spencer's. Regardless, she loved it, and she wrapped it round her tightly now to keep out the chill.

She was not all that surprised to see a large black car parked near the steps. Standing next to an open rear door was a lady chauffeur, in her forties Maggie reckoned, dressed in a black suit, tie and a hat with a flat crown and short brim.

The woman smiled as Maggie stepped off the bottom step. In turn, Maggie tried to blank her as she set off towards the terminal with Dingo. Unfortunately, judging by the line of passengers heading off, they would have to go past the car to get there.

'Mrs Matheson?' the chauffeur called as Maggie walked towards the car.

Maggie's eyes took a sudden interest in the baggage being unloaded off the other side of the plane. 'Do you think they put our cases on, Dingo love? It wouldn't be the first time my luggage has ended up somewhere else.'

'Don't know. Guess we'll find out when we get to the baggage hall.'

'Mrs Matheson… Mrs Matheson?' The chauffeur had moved round to the boot now, just as two large cases were being wheeled over by a baggage handler. A click and the lid rose gently, ready to accommodate the load. Under the chauffeur's direction, the handler began to lift them in.

'Oi!' Maggie said, walking towards the back of the car with Dingo in hot pursuit. 'Those are our cases!'

They definitely were. Standard black, Dingo had insisted on painting *Maggs* and *Dingo* onto each case using some old white paint he had been reluctant to throw away that had been sitting in one of his outhouses back on the ranch. Maggie had been horrified at the concept and his calligraphy, especially since much of the paint had now peeled off, leaving just *aggs* and *Di*.

'I certainly hope so, Mrs Matheson, and Dingo, isn't it?' the chauffeur asked, tipping the peak of her cap towards the large Australian.

'Hey, if she's Mrs Matheson, why don't I get called Mr Parfitt?'

Maggie stopped next to the car, turned to him, reached up and prodded his bottom lip back in. 'Because you don't give a snake's backside about formality… Mr Dingo. Now, help me get these cases out of the boot and we can be on our way.'

She was distracted by a purring sound, as the back window of the car came down. Inside, staring straight ahead, was a man in his late thirties, Maggie reckoned, wearing dark glasses. Without looking at her, he said: 'Do get in, Maggie.'

'And you are?' Names she struggled with; faces never. Even profiles wearing dark glasses, sitting in the dark interior of a car. This was a profile she had not come across before.

The man turned towards her, the new angle revealing a very shiny, bald head,

'Blimey,' said Dingo out of the corner of his mouth. 'The glare on that! Bet that takes a lot of buffing. His arm must ache more than a wallaby's ears at a Barry Manilow concert.'

The man's face remained impassive. Now she had a good look at it, Maggie thought he was closer to fifty than forty. With angular cheekbones, pale skin, thin lips and a pointed chin which had a small scar on the right-hand side, he had a face she would remember for sure. She wanted to see his eyes; they would tell whether he was someone she could trust. From what she had seen so far, it wasn't promising.

'My name is Quentin Stockley. Foreign Office.' He spoke in clipped tones, Eton, likely. *Faux Eton, more likely, Maggs*, she told herself. It sounded too forced.

'I would say that it's nice to meet you, Mr Stockley, but since you and your chauffeur seem intent on stealing our bags, I'm inclined to reserve judgement on that front.'

'Oh, we're not intending to take away your bags. Not without the two of you, anyway.'

'Kidnapping too, Mr Stockley? Is that how they keep people busy in the Foreign Office these days?'

'Come now, Maggie. You know as well as I do that when your country calls, the infamous and loyal Maggie Matheson will always respond.'

'I am retired, Mr Stockley. Twice. Not even calls I didn't take from my son and great-grandson could persuade me back to work for the Service. As tempting as it might be to go in a car with a man I've never met before who works for a department I have never worked for before, we will decline. Please unload our bags and we will be on our way.'

'No, Maggie. I can't do that.'

'Dingo, love, can you give me a hand to get the bags out? Or perhaps we can ask that baggage handler to help?'

She turned around to find him, but the handler had gone. The passengers had also all filed past now, the last of them disappearing into the terminal. Apart from the handlers on the far side of the plane, they were alone on the tarmac.

'I'm sorry you feel that way, Maggie,' the man continued. His tone had changed, and Maggie noticed a sudden edge to an accent that wasn't present before. 'Perhaps this…'

Maggie held up a hand. 'No, don't say it,' she said. 'You're going to say, "Perhaps this might persuade you," and then you're going to poke the barrel of a gun at me through the window.'

21

'Correct.' Sure enough, the gun appeared. 'Now, shall we?'

Maggie looked nervously at Dingo and was about to insist that they leave him and just take her when he marched off around the other side of the car and started to get in.

'Come on, Maggs,' he said over the top of the car. 'Let's get this bloody thing over and done with before I freeze my knackers off.'

Chapter 4

Security was not a problem. Whatever clearance Stockley had, it was high enough to get him and them out of Heathrow without being challenged. Barriers went up and officials stood aside as their car approached. Soon, they were on the M4, heading into London.

Maggie and Dingo sat opposite Stockley, hand in hand, while their kidnapper looked out of the window, his hand resting casually on the gun in his lap. Barely a word had been spoken, except for when the chauffeur pointed out, rather too cheerily in the circumstances Maggie felt, that there were drinks and snacks available in the cabinet to their right. She had introduced herself as 'Kim, their driver for today.' Her casual chirpiness either suggested she was very familiar with the methods her boss was using and was going along with some sort of psychological game, or she was always like this. Maggie was all for positivity, but not negative positivity when people said things like, 'Have a nice day,' as they pulled the trigger.

She felt a squeeze of the hand which she reciprocated. Here he was – her Dingo Derek – with her again. Supporting her, loving her, being there for her as she took them on another adventure. He was her rock, while she kept taking them to a hard place. The bit between was supposed to be an awkward spot, but it seemed quite inviting at the moment – a place where she was not too reliant on Dingo, and not sitting with him in the back of the car facing a man with a gun.

She could have asked where they were heading, but she didn't want to give Stockley the pleasure of being deliberately evasive or coy about it. He seemed the sort of person who liked to have the upper hand. The fact that he had barely looked at them since they got in suggested that he knew he was in control. Besides, she had a pretty good idea where they were heading: the Russian embassy.

She was right. They glided effortlessly through the London traffic and within an hour of landing, they were passing through the gates of the embassy in Kensington Palace Gardens.

The car drove down a ramp to an underground carpark where they were met by two burly gentlemen standing side-by-side, both, judging by the bulges in their black jackets, armed. With practised precision, they split – one walking around the vehicle to open the door nearest to Dingo, the other to open the one by

Stockley. His gun was out of sight now, not needed with all the security around.

Chauffeur Kim stayed in the car and drove off once they had all got out. Stockley led them up some steps and through a set of double doors which opened automatically. Maggie glanced behind her and quickly pulled her eyes to the front as she realised the taller of the two men on security was a) directly behind her and b) so was his crotch. When had she become so small that her eyeline was almost at the same height as men's crotches?

It was a conundrum to ponder for another day as they were led through a great marble hall with extravagant glass chandeliers and walls adorned with paintings of stern-looking militarily-attired men, past a grand wooden staircase which could have accommodated several sets of singing Von Trapp families, and into a conference room, white-walled, grey-carpeted and with a long table made up of eight smaller ones pushed together. Purchased, by the look of them, from a Swedish furniture store and assembled from components out of a box marked with an abundance of umlauts, it was disappointing. But what had she expected? A 50-foot table made from a single piece of mahogany placed on a red Persian carpet, a row of tanks and missile launchers on either side and the current head of the KGB, and former agent, Andrei Volkov, sitting at the end, stroking a snow leopard on his lap?

She was almost correct. Volkov was at the end, minus the snow leopard, but not in person. Instead, he peered out from a large television screen with a backdrop of the red buildings and ornate turrets of Moscow's Red Square. Slumped shoulders, red cheeks (presumably to match the buildings) and white hair, he had aged. About five years her junior, Maggie would have put him ten years older. High office clearly weighed heavily on him.

She had seen him on TV, but this was a closeup – and Maggie made it an even closer closeup by walking straight up to him, while Stockley and the two security men stood to attention, just inside the entrance.

Well, Maggs, she thought, *looks like you're well and truly committed now.*

So much for re-retirement.

She stopped a few feet short of the TV screen. With hands on hips, she looked at him sternly before saying, 'What's all this about, Andrei? Dragging me across London like this. I should be standing at the station with hundreds of other weary travellers, waiting for the Heathrow Express not to turn up.'

There was an audible gasp from the end of the room. It hadn't come from Dingo; he was right next to her. She felt his hand on her shoulder.

'Is this who I think it is, Maggs?'

She turned to face him, hands still wedged on her hips. 'Do you think it's Andrei Volkov, head of the KGB and the man I was talking about?'

'Yeah. Shouldn't you, er… well, it's not for me to say, I suppose, but shouldn't you speak to him with a little more decorum?'

'Decorum? You've read and seen the news about what his department gets up to, haven't you?'

'Yeah, well, I guess so, but…'

'Yes, well, enough said. But I don't suppose I've been brought here today to talk about world events, have I, Andrei?'

She turned back to the screen. Volkov raised an eyebrow and one corner of his lips curled up. It wasn't even a half smile, but it was enough for Maggie to recognise something of the KGB agent she had crossed swords with all those years ago.

'Maggie Matheson, how are you, my old friend?' he said in flawless English with hardly a trace of an accent.

Volkov was renowned for insisting all negotiations with diplomats and his equivalents in other countries were carried out in Russian, despite his fluency in English. Oxford educated, he refused, publicly at least, to speak English. There had been a famous incident a few years ago when the US Secretary of State had said hello to him and he had turned to his interpreter with a quizzical look to request a translation.

'Well, I'm gagging for a cuppa, for starters. What sort of kidnappers do you have working for you these days, Andrei?'

'You have not been kidnapped, Maggie.'

'Oh well, if that's the case, I'll say goodbye and thanks for the lift into town. If Mr Stockley could drop us off at the nearest underground station, we will be on our way.'

'Not just yet. We have business to discuss.' He turned to the side and barked something in Russian. A moment later there was a ping from the back of the room, followed by the sound of a door opening and shutting. Maggie turned round; Stockley was no longer there.

'That'll be our tea on the way,' she whispered in response to Dingo's raised eyebrows. 'The Gulag next for Stockley, unless he gets back here double-quick.'

'Seems a bit harsh.'

Maggie shrugged. 'Andrei always liked his tea. We shared many a cuppa negotiating prisoner swaps, amongst other things, in Berlin. A bit too casual a way of dealing with people's lives and futures, I guess, but we got the job done. Laid the groundwork for our superiors to make the final decisions. I always supplied the teabags – good, old-fashioned breakfast tea.'

'Drinking British tea and with that Oxford education, makes you wonder why he's so against speaking English. Practically a pom!'

There was a loud 'Ahem' from the screen which brought Maggie back to the task in hand.

'I am still here, you realise,' Volkov said ominously. 'And I do know what a pom is, Mr. Parfitt. I can tell you; I'm not keen on being accused of being like one.'

It was said in such a manner to make Dingo almost stand to attention, then he leaned in and said to him, 'Don't blame you. Neither would I.' And then more quietly to Maggie, 'At least he used my surname, unlike Stockley's chauffeur. Respect is all I ask for. It's not much, is it?'

'Ah, the tea has arrived,' Maggie interrupted, her ears, just like with the click of a Glock 17 pistol, were tuned to the clink of a teacup from 500 yards away. 'That was extremely quick.'

Stockley entered carrying a tray with a chintzy matching teapot, cups, saucers, milk jug and sugar bowl. He was sweating and his smile seemed a little forced as he placed the tray on the table next to them.

'Enjoy,' he half-growled to Maggie, before standing to attention again and giving a formal bow of the head in the direction of the screen.

'Thank you so much, Mr. Stockley. Now, if this is good old-fashioned breakfast tea, Andrei, perhaps we can sit down and you can tell me what all this about.'

Chapter 5

'You have heard about our mutual friend, Mr. Steinman, Maggie? He has left his period of solitude.'

'Indeed, yes. He is claiming political asylum, I understand. A diplomatic problem. Perhaps that is something Mr Stockley can help with since he works for the Foreign Office?'

'I don't want to teach you your job, Maggs, but I think that's just a cover.' Dingo's attempts to intervene quietly and helpfully were made with good intentions, she had no doubt. But being neither quiet nor helpful, they ended up being just interventions; interventions she could do without.

'Very droll, Maggie,' Volkov said, showing no signs that it was. 'Now, you know Steinman has information about me which could be – how shall I put this…?'

'A pain in the proverbial arse?' Dingo piped up.

Maggie smiled. Perhaps she should reassess her husband's interjections. Occasionally having a disruptor on your side did no harm, in her experience.

'That is one way to put it, Mr. Parfitt. At this point, perhaps you should finish your tea elsewhere so that Maggie and I can discuss these *pains* in more detail.'

Dingo sat back and folded his arms. 'I'm stayin'. Maggie and I have no secrets.'

'We both know that's not true, Mr. Parfitt. She was a spy for many decades. I do know she likes to chat, but not even she could have told you all the secrets she knows. How long have you two been together now? Eighteen months, two weeks and four days, I make it. Does that sound right?'

Volkov may be older, but he had not lost any of his edge. Detail had always been his strong point. Especially detail about his enemies. Throwing in facts no person should know other than the person themselves, unnerved the best agents, and – from what

Maggie had heard on the world stage – politicians alike.

'Five days, actually, Mr. Volkov. Make sure you get your facts right.' Then, through the corner of his mouth once more: 'To be honest, Maggs, I haven't a scooby-bloody-do how long it's been. Sorry.'

'Thank you for your support, Dingo-love, and do stay. But perhaps leave this to me from now on. I'm sure Mr Volkov won't mind. Now, Andrei. Wouldn't it be easier for you, bearing in mind what I know, if you simply killed me and Oliver Steinman? A drop of Novichok in a drink or something would have done it.'

'Maggie, Maggie, Maggie... I don't even know what Novichok is. Something poisonous I assume from your tone? No, that is not the way we Russians do things. I would prefer a diplomatic solution... an unofficial one, between you and me.'

'Is that possible? I mean, I've kept my side of the bargain for all this time by being quiet, but I can't speak for Oliver Steinman.'

'But you could, Maggie Matheson. Speak to him and then for him. I don't want this to be an embarrassment to the Western governments.'

'For you, more like.' Maggie took a sip of her tea. 'Nice cuppa your Mr Stockley makes, by the way. He'll go far in the Foreign Office.'

Volkov shrugged a shrug which Maggie knew all too well. They had played many diplomatic games way back when. A series of jabs, blocks and counter-jabs between the two of them had invariably ended in a decent outcome that suited all parties. They were in the middle of another such contest here.

'I am a fair man, always thinking about our foreign friends.'

'I don't know where Oliver is, Andrei. Even if I did, I'm not sure I should help you. You have a lot to lose.'

There was a flicker and Volkov's expression darkened. It was not lost on Maggie who knew she was playing an even more dangerous game than the ones they had played in Berlin. More was at stake. Much more. He recovered quickly and smiled. 'Let's just say, if you do what I ask, you and your country will benefit enormously. If you don't…'

'The threat, with the smile, I note – so late in the conversation, Andrei? Your methods have changed from the old days. You used to get that in right at the beginning.'

Her comment elicited a chuckle. It was at that point she decided she best play along, despite her reservations. For all his faults, Volkov would always strike a bargain. She would much rather be dealing with him than some of his predecessors. *Better the devil you know, Maggs.*

'Ok, if I did decide to help, how would I go about it?'

'We will agree what should be said… and not be said. You will relay this to him.'

'How? I don't know where he is.'

'Your Secret Service has him hidden away at a secure location.'

'Do they? Okay, Andrei. I'm prepared to listen to what you'd like me to say to Oliver. Then I might consider speaking to him. No promises though.'

That smile again. 'That is good, Maggie Matheson.'

'I assume you know where the Secret Service's secure, secret location is?'

'Of course. We will text you the address.'

Dingo sat forward with his hand up towards Volkov. 'Text it? Don't do that, for Chrissakes. Not if you want her to actually read the bloody thing.'

This time it was just themselves and Kim in the car. Stockley had been left clearing up the teacups and they had not seen him since. Their luggage, Kim explained, had been sent on and would be waiting for them when they got home. They were heading for an address in Clerkenwell, North London, an area Maggie was not at all familiar with. Fortunately, Kim, she assured them, was on it, with the Satnav being 'her guide and friend'.

Maggie couldn't but like Kim. And it wasn't just her cheery manner.

'Do you find being a double agent tricky, dear?' she enquired casually as they stopped at a zebra crossing to let a father pushing a toddler in a pram cross the road. The toddler had chocolate splurged around his chops and he gave a cheery wave as he was wheeled past.

Maggie noticed a whitening of Kim's knuckles in response, but she recovered quickly by waving back at the child, before accelerating away. 'A double agent?' she said, tilting her head towards the back. 'I wouldn't know what one was, even if one slapped me around the face with a copy of the Times and a red rose, then introduced themselves as Kim Philby. Sorry; bad example with him being called Kim too. My surname's not Philby either.'

It was a good answer and Maggie had to laugh.

'Maybe not a double, but a triple with you initially pretending to work for the Foreign Office with Stockley, then being a driver for the Russian embassy, but actually working undercover for the Service. And the agent bit only applying to the last part with the other roles being driving jobs. Unless you are the elusive quadruple; an agent for the Russians, pretending to be a British agent, pretending to be a driver for the Russian embassy, pretending to be a driver for the Foreign Office.'

Maggie noticed Dingo push his hand over his face and shake his head. He didn't say anything which was an indication of how tired he probably was after the flight and subsequent events. His eyes started to close. She would love to do the same, but she needed to stay alert for a while longer yet.

'I'm not an agent for anyone, Mrs Matheson. I…'

'You don't need to worry, dear. You've done your job. Kept Stockley in check, no doubt, and fed back any titbits you heard. We're both on the same side.'

'Joshua said I was not to tell you.'

'Oh, he's only saying that to help you keep up the pretence. I used to do the same with the double agents I managed. Stay in role for as long as you can, even amongst your own. It's a mindset: the more you think and act like the other side, the more convincing you are. It's to protect the agent. Is this your first role as a double agent?'

'Yes.'

'You're very good.'

'Not that good; you saw through me.'

'I see through most people, dear. These specs of mine are x-ray.' She waggled one corner of her glasses and saw a smile form in the rearview mirror, the knuckles on the wheel relaxing at the same time. 'The important thing is that the other side doesn't know.'

'I switched Stockley's bullets for blanks. You were perfectly safe.'

'I know, dear, and I'm grateful. You're compromised now unless you switched them back?'

'Done. He left his gun in the car. No guns inside the embassy building unless you're security staff.'

'Then you will live to fight another day. Drop me off, as instructed, and then head back. Unless there are listening bugs in the car?'

'No. Stockley insisted I sweep the car whenever I drive him anywhere. He's acting as an agent for the Iranians. A sideline his Russian bosses don't know about that's earning him a few extra quid.'

Maggie nodded. Corruption was rife in the spy game. It was a good job she had people she could rely on. Joshua and Bill, as expected, had been looking out for her. 'Be careful, Kim.'

'I will, Mrs Matheson. Right, you relax now. We are about fifteen minutes away, depending on traffic.'

Maggie knew that with London traffic that could be anything up to an hour. Perhaps she could afford a few minutes of not being alert after all.

Chapter 6

Flat 73 was on the eighth floor of a tower block, one of several in an estate, similar to the one she and her first husband, Frankie, had lived on briefly in the East End after they were married. That had been run down then, even though it was new. Poverty was a difficult thing to tackle and there were signs of it on this estate too with graffiti rife. Not the artistic kind; more the 'I hate the Filth' and 'Dawn hearts Phil' kind. Some thoughtful souls had put a couple of cars onto bricks, presumably to stop the undercarriage going rusty on the wet floor, Maggie thought wryly. There were a few boarded-up windows on one of the ground-floor flats next to where Kim dropped Maggie and Dingo. Nearby, was one bicycle wheel with a lock attaching it to a railing. It had started to drizzle – the sort of rain that didn't look much but soaked unprotected pedestrians, foolhardy enough to be out and about, within minutes.

Maggie shivered as she got out of the car and waved Kim off while she still had four wheels to drive on. Dingo put a protective arm around her shoulder and together they headed for the entrance to Thomas Patterson House, hoping against hope that it had a working lift.

'You rarely see these tower blocks named after women,' Maggie said as they entered a dimly lit entrance hall. The peeling paint and rubbish under the stairwell added to the ambience of neglect; discarded syringes and empty vodka bottles signs of an even bigger problem.

'Not many statues either,' said Dingo. 'Though I'm sure they'll commission one for you, Maggs.'

'I'd like that. Made of pumice stone so I could be transported easily from one place to another. Change my view now and again.'

'Strewth! The lift is buggered. Eight floors, isn't it? Why are they holding him up there?'

'You can stay here if you like, Dingo love.' She was worried. He had been on a strict exercise regime since his stroke, but it hadn't included vertical climbs of one-hundred-plus steps. 'Probably best if…'

He didn't let her finish. 'We're in this together, Maggs. I kinda knew what a bloody pain in the arse you were going to be when we hooked up.'

'You say the nicest things, you old romantic you.' But she was pleased. Marrying Dingo had been one of her best decisions.

'Are you sure we're not being set up by the Russians here? I mean, you've only got their word that Steinman is here.'

'Am I sure we're not being set up by the Russians? No. It's highly probable.'

Maggie could see that Dingo was about to do one of his blusters, a process which involved a whole series of unintelligible, angry words, backed up by a lot of heavy breathing. Heavy breathing that would be far better used for tackling the stairs, so she grabbed his arm, stepped over a pool of vomit and started the long climb.

She was on the third floor, about to turn to face the next set of steps, when she heard – and felt – the explosion. A bang so loud it rattled doors, windows and teeth. In her younger days, her instinct would have been to throw herself to the floor, but these days, her knee and hip joints ruled the rest of her body with an iron rod and stood creakily firm. Instead, her back took the strain as she bent forward and thrust her arm in front of her head. Dingo was behind, still tackling the last couple of steps to floor three. When she looked behind, he was sprawled out – his feet three stairs down, his belly and arms flat on the floor.

'Dingo!' she called, stooping down.

He immediately lifted his head. 'I'm okay, Maggs. I was in this position already, taking a breather. You okay?'

'I'm fine. It came from somewhere above.'

'Eighth floor?'

'I wouldn't be surprised.' Her stomach lurched. 'If Bill and Joshua were with Steinman…' She couldn't finish the sentence.

Dingo used his powerful arms to push himself up into a press-up position, then grabbed the handrail to haul himself to his feet. Standing below her, they were similar heights. Leaning forward, he held out one arm and pulled her in for a hug. She went in willingly, a big part of her needing the comfort, but her mind was elsewhere worrying about her boys. Were Bill and Joshua even in the building? Was Steinman? Volkov had sent her here – she could have been done away with long before now, as could Steinman have been since Volkov knew where he was – but perhaps this was a chance to kill two birds with one stone. The old classic, 'a domestic gas explosion' given as the cause of the blast. If that was the case, it had been mistimed. She and Dingo were a good five minutes away from the flat.

She eased herself away from Dingo. 'I have to go up, see what the situation is.' She didn't want to at all, of course. It could be messy.

'Is it time to call in some help, Maggs? I'm not bein' funny but that coulda been a bomb meant for you. There could be someone else around here to make sure the job is finished properly.'

The distant sound of sirens confirmed that help was on its way, but Maggie knew Dingo was referring to more specialist help.

'You're right, of course, but I have to see what's happened.'

The sounds of doors opening, panicked voices, and the scream of a baby, signalled the start of an exodus down the stairs. Their way up would not be straightforward. Dingo nodded and grabbed her hand. If she was going to climb against the tide of people leaving the building, she would need a hefty-outbacker-sized shield.

Despite human obstacles and gravity against them, they moved more quickly than before, the urgency of the situation driving both on.

One elderly man grabbed her arm as she brushed past. 'Don't go up there, you stupid cow!' he said. 'There's been an explosion on the eighth.'

Combining concern with insult was quite a knack, given the situation. It took her back to her Eastend childhood when people didn't mince their words, yet had hearts of gold.

She let go of Dingo's hand. 'You sure it was the eighth?'

'Course I am. I live on the eighth, three doors down. Took me clean out me chair. Nearly spilled me Guinness. Had to down it quickly before I left. Don't like that. Can only afford one a day, what with my Babestation subscription and all. I like to sit down and savour both.'

Maggie's mind might have boggled, had she not been focussed on accumulating information.

'Did you see anyone come out?' She and Dingo were pinned against the wall as a man and woman carrying two children each pushed between them and the old man. They were in danger of being a hindrance if they stayed where they were.

'No one was coming out of that place. The flames... Now, if you'll excuse me, I need to get to the Albion. After Babestation and explosions, I've got quite the thirst.'

They continued up, through the fourth, fifth, and sixth. The number of people leaving thinned out, with some people, Maggie surmised, opting to stay put, perhaps. How wise that was remained to be seen.

On the sixth, they walked out of the stairwell to the shared balcony which ran the length of each floor and allowed access to the flats. She leaned out and looked up to the left and then right. Flames licking the outside of a flat on the right-hand corner made their destination clear. She looked down just as three fire engines screeched to a halt. Several police cars and ambulances were already there and she could hear instructions being shouted as people were shepherded away. Soon, the place would be swarming with emergency workers.

She felt a pang of guilt. After all; these people were in danger because she was here. It quickly changed to anger as she cursed how so-called diplomats and the political elite affected ordinary people's lives. Volkov and his ilk had a lot to answer for on a micro-level as well as on the macro-global one.

Use the anger, Maggs. Use it! She needed all the help she could get to climb those last two floors.

It helped. Dingo, now urging her on from behind, was like a man possessed as he kept pace. Eighty-four… she felt like she was fifty-five as she bounded up the last few steps and arrived on the eighth.

Out on the balcony, she could feel the heat from the flames as they carefully approached Flat 73, peering through the windows as they passed. All were dark or had curtains pulled, doors firmly shut. The threat of the fire spreading was real so she hoped everyone had got out safely. As they neared, she realised that the old man they had passed was right; no one inside could survive such a blaze, surely. An early escape would have been the only option but as she knew all too well, Russian assassinations – if this was what it was – rarely came with advanced warnings.

Ten metres away was about as close as they could stand. All she could do was… well, hope that Volkov had misled her about the location of Steinman. Or that if Steinman, Bill and Joshua – or anyone else for that matter – had been in there they had somehow survived and got out.

As it turned out, someone did get out, but their chance of survival was poor. Very poor indeed. Maggie looked on horrified as a human fireball crashed through the door of flat 73, straight into and over the balcony.

She looked over the edge as it plummeted down eight stories and landed with a thud on the ground below.

Chapter 7

Twenty minutes later, Maggie watched on from below, sunk into a plastic chair that had materialised from somewhere, along with a blanket from a similar unknown source. Dingo was in a chair next to her. A stream of water was being trained on the flat they had not long stood outside. Around them, emergency workers were active supporting people who had escaped. A TV camera crew had turned up. How, so quickly, she did not know.

Maggie was not easily shocked, though there were some notable exceptions.

The price of first-class stamps, now that *was* a shock. The fact that bank tellers stood next to podiums, and not behind glass, wearing signs saying they were happy to help in places that looked like the set of a TV travel show, that shocked her too. How far her feet were from her hands, despite her body having shrunk in her later years, was another example.

But blood, gore, and violence didn't shock her. She had seen so much that she had become immune. Or so she thought. Seeing someone burning and falling to their death had been a new experience; not a pleasant one, and she felt numb all over.

Dingo was staring blankly at the water jet with his mouth open. He would need keeping an eye on – they both would – since the effects of shock could be traumatic. She decided to get him talking. It might help them both.

'The firefighters who helped us down were kind, weren't they?' It was met with silence. 'Efficient too. No mucking about.' Still no response. 'The ambulance crew have triaged us. Said there had been some falls as people rushed out. An elderly couple broke an arm each.' Nothing. 'Someone will be back to check on us... Shouldn't be long... Dingo, love, are you listening?... Dingo?'

She shook his arm gently, then more forcibly when he still failed to respond. She leaned over and clicked her fingers in front of his eyes. She was a hopeless clicker (online and offline). A jellyfish wearing mittens jumping into a sack filled with cotton wool would make a louder noise. However, the movement in front of his eyes knocked him out of his stupor. He looked at her, then back up at flat 73.

'It – she, he – was on fire, Maggs.' His voice, usually so robust, sounded distant and weak. 'Then they went over.'

A blue tent had been erected to their left; the spot where the body – it had to be just a body – landed.

'I know, love. It's awful.'

'How could...' His voice faltered before he found the wherewithal to continue, a tear forming in his eye. 'How could someone do that? You reckoned it was a bomb or something? Done deliberately. How could someone do that, knowing the pain that could cause?'

She nodded. 'The investigation team will find out for sure whether it was deliberate, but us being there,

Volkov's involvement... let's say it's unlikely to be a coincidence.'

'Do you think... do you think Joshua and Bill were in there? Could it have been one of them who... who...'

She couldn't contemplate it. The thought that they could have been in there, one of them could have been the fireball. The horror, of having survived the blast and then not being able to get out. Maggie took a deep breath. She had to hold it together, not just for her sake but for Dingo's too.

She could not keep exposing him to danger. This was her life, her job, her fault. He should be in Frampton, supping a quiet pint at the local after a walk, a Sunday roast acting as ballast in his stomach, before going back to their flat and falling asleep in front of the telly. Instead, he was running upstairs to witness horrendous sights that no human should ever witness.

As for either Bill or Joshua being there in a body bag at the bottom of a building in Clerkenwell, the other burnt to a cinder inside the flat, she had to tell herself that it was no more than a possibility.

And ignore that part of her brain that told her it was a distinct one.

Booking into a hotel in London seemed the most sensible option until they sorted out what was going on. So, avoiding too much police scrutiny, they asked one of the residents to book a taxi and told the driver to drop them off at the nearest hotel. That nearest one was a bit of a two-star dive, but their room was clean and would do.

Maggie's phone had been switched off in her handbag since they had landed, as had Dingo's. She hadn't been able to face switching it on since the explosion for fear of what might come up... or rather, not come up. The thought that there would not be a comforting message from Bill or Joshua to say they were okay was not something she felt she could face after what they had just witnessed. No news, in most cases, was good news. In this case, her gut told her the reverse.

But she couldn't put it off any longer. With late afternoon looming and Dingo crashed out on the bed, snoring away, it was time to see.

She took a deep breath and... spent the next two minutes trying to work out why nothing was happening. They had charged their phones on the plane, or at least she thought they had. Perhaps her phone was broken? The frustration with new technology not doing what she considered to be the simplest of things added to her anxiety.

Another minute was spent searching for Dingo's phone through his trouser pockets, cursing his insistence on wearing cargos with hundreds of the blasted things. Until she remembered that since they would be travelling on the Underground, he said he would keep it in his sock, out of the reach of muggers. This was a pointless precaution in Maggie's opinion. With so many pockets to choose from, a mugger would have needed the patience of a saint to find anything on Dingo. The chances of that mugger a) having many saintly attributes and b) Dingo allowing anyone other than Maggie to pat him down for a full minute without clouting them, seemed slim.

It was in his sock and charged, so she switched it on. His passcode was easy to remember – four, three, two, one: 'Because the hacking bastards won't think to do the numbers backwards' – and she was in.

There were no comforting messages from Joshua or Bill. Only one message from an unknown number.

She opened it.

Tell her to be at the bottom of Tower Bridge, Southbank side. 7pm. ALONE, or else.

Immediately, another message arrived, presumably based on the fact that Dingo's had been read.

And tell her to switch on her bloody phone.

The first message was almost standard spy talk: an instruction; a place and time; a threat.

The second message was odd. The use of the vernacular 'bloody' with the instruction to switch on her phone was familiar. Someone she knew quite well who would threaten her then. Given her history, it could be anyone.

Well, there was only one way to find out. She had just over an hour to get across town. With a quick peck on Dingo's forehead, she grabbed her handbag and left quietly, relieved that she had left her knitting and needles in there. She might well need them.

She had been on the Underground train enough times and was experienced enough in covert techniques to know when she was being followed.

She had spotted in the foyer of Farringdon Underground Station a man in his forties wearing jeans and a bomber jacket with a brown scarf, standing by a ticket machine, looking at his phone. She caught a glance in her direction before his head went down again. Clumsy by him. Classic error. Always scan around the target. Use peripheral vision to confirm whereabouts. Never – never – catch their eye, not even for a split second.

He kept within range on the platform before taking up a standing position on the train behind two construction workers by the doors to her left.

The second followed along shortly. A woman, possibly of Asian origin, in her sixties sitting almost directly opposite. She arrived one stop along the Circle Line at Barbican. To begin with, Maggie did not particularly suspect her. She settled in and then opened a paperback to read. Every time Maggie scanned the carriage her head was focussed on the book. Except it wasn't. Maggie wore bifocals but this did not mean she struggled to see. Quite the opposite. With them, she had near-perfect vision, and this meant that when she was on high alert, as she was now, she could hone in on the most subtle of idiosyncrasies. This woman's eyes were not following a text, despite the occasional page turn. Her eyes barely moved. Unlike the man at the Farringdon Tube Station, her peripheral vision was hard at work – too hard, too obvious.

Who was she dealing with here? Two tails on her and both clearly so to a seasoned spy such as Maggie. It was almost amateurish.

Amateurish, Maggs, or a warning?

Either way, she had made her move. They – whoever 'they' were – had also made theirs.

Chapter 8

It was six-thirty by the time Maggie walked up the steps from the Underground – fighting commuters this time rather than fleeing residents – and headed for Tower Bridge. She could take her time to cross London's iconic landmark, safe in the knowledge that with the crowds on it, she was unlikely to be in any immediate danger. Besides, whoever was tailing her was probably more interested in finding out what she was doing than throwing her into the Thames. Her tails had either blended into the throng or had been replaced by others. No matter. For better or worse, she would find out soon enough what the next step was in this case.

Case, Maggs? Is that what this is? Another case? Another brown folder – or modern digital equivalent – marked top secret, opened by someone in Whitehall to be shut when the case was closed, her name to be commented on and forgotten ten years from now?

Ten years? Who was she kidding? Ten minutes, more like.

And what about the human fireball? How would they be remembered? Whoever that was – friend or foe – didn't deserve to die like that. Probably didn't deserve to die at all. Would they be anything more than a statistic? Were any of them more than that, especially to someone ambitious like Volkov? Ambition and ruthlessness were what it took for people to become head of the KGB. But he wouldn't have become head – would likely not remain as such – if the secret that she and Steinman shared became public knowledge.

That meeting 36 years ago… she remembered it well. Steinman, in the eyes of the GDR and the Soviets, epitomised the communist way. His art was lauded – big, bold sculptures of the heroes of the struggle against Western tyranny. Lauded, yet his work was abstract, which meant it could be interpreted any way people wanted. Steinman knew what his art represented, and it had nothing to do with what the powers in the GDR and beyond thought it was. His figures railed against the oppression, but it suited him for others to see it otherwise. He went along with it, mixed with the powerful and rich, said the right things or shrugged enigmatically when people discussed his art, allowing people to think it was something it wasn't. All the while, he listened and learned and passed on information to the West.

But he had wanted to get out of the situation. Why? Because the KGB had been onto him. It had been down to Maggie, as one of his handlers, to get him out safely, but she had needed Volkov's help to do it. And why would Volkov help? Well, by that stage, those teas-for-two with Volkov had already occasionally become teas-for-three with Steinman. Then they became teas-for-two without Maggie. Then they became teas-for-two without Maggie and without the tea.

Maggie gripped the stone handrail that wound down the steps to the hustle and bustle of the Southbank. There, commuters mixed with tourists and locals going about their early evening business on what was no longer a wet autumnal day, just a chilly one.

One individual was sitting outside a bar under the cover of the bridge arches, a black-gloved hand occasionally moving a pint of bitter to his lips. Dressed in a sheepskin coat, a red scarf and a soft, flat cap, a cigar between finger and thumb on his other hand, he would have blended in perfectly with the crowd, had they all also been dressed like 1970s football managers.

He motioned for Maggie to join him. 'You don't look that surprised to see me, Maggie.'

'I'm not. Your text gave it away. No one uses the word bloody anymore, except English people of my generation and Russian KGB agents. You're head of it, your dirty hands all over our social media. I thought you'd be a bit more tuned in, Andrei.'

Volkov raised an eyebrow in response. 'Have a drink with me, Maggie?'

'No, thank you. I'm here for business. You didn't need to put the "or else" threat on the text.'

'Sorry about that. I think it gets added automatically on all KGB correspondence.'

Volkov still had a sense of humour, but she was in no mood to laugh.

'I thought you were in Moscow.'

'In my office overlooking Red Square? It actually looks out onto a very dull brick wall. I was brought to you by the power of green screen.'

Green screen – Maggie hadn't the foggiest what he was talking about. Anyway, this was small talk; she wanted to cut to the chase. 'What are you doing over here, Andrei? Making sure your assassins are doing their job properly?'

'We don't use assassins. But if you are referring to the explosion in Clerkenwell…'

'Of course, I'm referring to that,' she snapped. She wondered whether anyone else could hear her heart thumping. 'Who was in there, Andrei? Who did you kill?'

'Perhaps if I told you there was no collateral damage?'

'What do you mean, no collateral damage?'

'Have a drink and I will explain.'

'No. Tell me what happened at the flat. Who did you murder this time?'

A fleeting expression of sadness crossed his eyes, but just as quickly it disappeared. 'Ah, here's your drink. I took the liberty of ordering you a G&T in anticipation you would prefer that to this disgusting glass of brown, warm liquid, you English call beer.'

A large stemmed glass appeared over her shoulder, the bowl full to the brim with ice and a slice, and what she assumed were the two most important ingredients of any G&T. She thanked the waitress, but she didn't want it. What she wanted was answers.

'You told me Steinman was being kept at the flat by some of our agents.'

'None of your agents were at the flat, Maggie. As I said: no collateral damage.' He sat forward. 'Ah, you are worried about your son and grandson, yes? They are part of your Service.'

'I'm worried about anyone who might have been blown up.' She could feel herself getting emotional. She didn't want that. As calmly as she could, she added, 'I've not heard from anyone since it happened.'

'Then it is your Service who is playing games with you. Not I... this time.'

'At least one person died. I saw them.' Once again, that flicker of emotion on Volkov's normally impassive face. 'Who was it?'

She watched him take another sip of his pint. He was doing a good job of hiding the fact it was disgusting, brown liquid. What he wasn't doing a good job of was hiding his emotions.

'It was Steinman, wasn't it?'

A barely perceptible nod. 'It was an accident.'

'Really?'

'Well, no. A deliberate accident, but not of my doing.'

'Why should I believe you?'

'Because you are still alive and well, sitting at a bar in London not drinking a gin and tonic.'

As much as she needed a drink, she was determined not to touch what was in front of her. He had mentioned games. Well, she had had enough of these games. Games were supposed to be fun but this one they were 'playing' was no fun at all. It was time to put a stop to this one, at least.

'That was Steinman? That's awful. The poor, poor man.'

It would take a while to get that horror scene out of her mind. She hadn't seen or had any contact with Steinman since he went into isolation, but it was someone she knew, which made it worse... if that was possible.

Volkov had turned his head away, concentrating on a spot somewhere in the middle of the Thames.

'Did you still love him, Andrei?' she asked softly.

For the first time since she had arrived, the cigar went to his lips. He looked over it at her before taking a long drag. His eyes squinted as he did so, reminding Maggie of the look he used to give her over the many teas they had shared all those years ago. Back then it had been mainly distrustful, other times trusting, and very occasionally – when Steinman was with them – joyous.

A pause as he inhaled, then he tipped his head back and blew the smoke into the air.

'I never stopped.'

It was the love that dared not speak its name – especially for an ambitious KGB agent with a reputation to uphold. 36 years later, it should be more acceptable. But not in Russia. And definitely not if you headed up an organisation known for its lack of tolerance.

The big secret. For Volkov, it was more devastating than any of the state ones Steinman gave to the West. But Volkov was no traitor. When his team found out Steinman was dealing in state secrets, he had to stop it. A simple bullet would have done the job. He and Maggie had come up with an alternative for his lover and friend and Steinman became a hermit.

'Why pretend you were in Moscow? Why send me to the flat?'

'I trusted you, Maggie.'

'Trusted me? Trusted me to do what?'

'To look after him.'

'You mean our lot weren't looking after him? But you said...'

'Your lot didn't know where he was. No one did. I couldn't trust anyone if I was to protect him. I arranged to bring him over to you. That's why I'm here. To oversee matters. I didn't do a very good job.'

It took a moment. She willed the cogs in her brain to see what – apart from a gin and tonic – was right in front of her.

'Your lot didn't know where he was either?'

'There are people in the Kremlin with very long memories. Oliver gave away secrets to the West. That, many think, is unforgivable. I hoped that by personally intervening I could hide him away from those out for revenge. Regrettably, I was wrong.'

'Let me get this right. You smuggled over a high-profile Russian dissident, hoping that an eighty-four-year-old retired spy with dodgy knees, hips and a very small flat by the seaside would be able to make him disappear? What did you think I would do? Put a doily over his head and hide him in the corner of my lounge?'

'I thought you could use your connections. Keep it in the family. I know you have people you can trust in the Service.'

So did she. But where were they?

'Andrei, this is crazy! What about those at the embassy who saw me? Surely, no one breaks wind in there without your president knowing about it. Then there's that rat, Stockley. He's a wrong-un.'

'That's where I was misguided, I fear. I'm getting old, Maggie. Making mistakes. Twenty years he has worked directly for me.'

'Making the tea? There's nothing wrong with making tea for a living – God knows, it would be my ideal job if I wasn't a spy – but you treated him like dirt when we were at the embassy, Andrei. He jumped when you told him to. I could see the fear in his eyes.'

'He obviously wasn't scared enough.' In response to Maggie's raised eyebrows, he continued: 'We do things differently in Russia, you should know that by now.'

'Your misjudgement caused the love of your life to be murdered.' *Ouch, Maggie! That was harsh, even for you.*

Volkov took another puff on his cigar. This time, Maggie doubted that it was the smoke from the cigar that was making his eyes water.

'What now? Oliver Steinman's dead. There's nothing I can do, so why am I here?'

'What is the expression you English use? To sort the wheat from the chaff?'

'What?'

'I have nothing much to live for now. My last case has gone, how you say, "Tits up." I've failed. Oliver is dead. I'm old and...' He let out a sigh. 'I've had enough of these games. Like you, perhaps? There are people in the Kremlin who don't like my methods. People whose methods are considerably more unlikeable than mine. We can't get all the chaff, Maggie, but perhaps some of it.'

'I've lured them to you, haven't I?'

'Almost certainly, yes.'

Before she could react, a voice intervened behind her: 'Oh, quite definitely, yes!'

She recognised that faux Eton accent straight away.

Chapter 9

As surprised as she was by developments, instinct kicked in. 'Mr Stockley,' she said as he joined them at the table. 'Is that a very – very – small gun in your pocket or are you just pleased to see me?'

It was a cheap shot, but it landed. Stockley gave a sickly smile before saying, 'Actually, it's a very – very – big gun, much like my… but that doesn't matter right now. What does matter is that you have lured me to the target, Andrei Volkov, who is now out in the open.'

'The target you are too ashamed to look at, Mr Stockley? Your boss?'

Stockley briefly flicked his eyes towards Volkov. 'He's not my boss any longer. I have orders. He is to be liquidated.'

'By you, along with the help you've brought with you, I see.'

'What?'

'Those two, there, who I saw on the Underground…' She pointed to the man and woman who had been following her. The woman was sitting with her back to them in an adjoining bar and the man was by the water's edge, taking an awfully long time to line up a picture of Tower Bridge. 'I believe the young men pretending to fix one of their bicycles over there are yours too, as is that juggler who keeps dropping his balls.'

'How did you…?'

'Then there's the guy sitting cross-legged on the floor holding the piece of cardboard with *I'm homeless* written on it, and the young couple kissing next to the steps. Not sure if they're both yours or whether the very attractive girl has found some lucky man to act as a foil at short notice.'

'But...'

'I assume you're intending to take Mr Volkov somewhere quiet to do the deed? I know this area very well and can recommend a place. If you follow the river that way...' Stockley followed her hand as she pointed east, allowing just enough time for the other hand to reach into her bag. '... Turn left past the Mexican restaurant, walk fifty yards and take a right. There's a very quiet alleyway where you won't be disturbed.'

'Well, Maggie Matheson, that sounds just fine. Because you'll be coming with us, you can show us the way.'

A patch on Stockley's bald head that Dingo had commented on at the airport gleamed in the light from an outdoor heater one of the waiting staff had just switched on nearby. He edged his chair closer and Maggie felt the butt of a gun under the table against her thigh.

'No, I think not,' she said.

'I think so. We Russians are very good at this sort of thing.'

'Russian, eh? What about your Iranian work? Does whoever you're working for in the Kremlin know about that?'

The blood seemed to drain from Stockley's face. This conversation was almost certainly being recorded, either with a bug on him or, more likely with sophisticated listening equipment from further away.

He started to bluster about what rubbish that was, but Maggie cut him short. Apart from Stockley's team, she had been busy spotting, in her periphery, other activity: the cavalry in the form of Joshua, Bill and others. *Better late than never, Maggs, I suppose.* Judging by the slight upturn of Volkov's lips, he had spotted them too.

It was time to end this before Stockley panicked and that gun went off.

'Both of you will get up now,' Stockley instructed, 'and head left towards that alley.' The gun, no longer against her thigh, would be pointing somewhere in the region of her guts, Maggie guessed.

'We could do that,' she said sweetly, 'but if you insisted, I would have to push my knitting needle which has already pierced that nice Burberry jacket of yours, through your no-doubt nicely tanned skin into your liver and out the other side.'

'You haven't got a knit... ohh, yes, you have. My gun would go off before...'

'Mine would be a quick death. Yours, however...' She glanced up and took in the developing – and amazingly quiet, unfussy scene – around her. As far as she could tell, all of Stockley's people were occupied by the flurry of agents Joshua and Bill had brought with them. The hustle and bustle of the Southbank continued to hustle and bustle, none the wiser that a major sting was in operation.

Her boys were so good at their jobs. Even if they were a bit late to the party.

Chapter 10

Maggie and Dingo were back home in Frampton. They had been for that walk; Dingo had had that pint and roast dinner at the local pub. And now he was about to settle into the sofa for that nap in front of the telly.

'Why do they fill the Sunday afternoon TV schedules with crap?' he exclaimed, angrily pressing buttons on the remote control.

'What does it matter if you're going to fall asleep in front of it anyway?'

'We pay a licence fee – we should be able to fall asleep in front of decent stuff. I'd watch the football if they didn't insist on just kicking away at the bloody thing rather than picking it up, clouting someone and then running with it.' He put the remote control down. 'I'll do what Sharon said I should do.

Agatha... Agatha ... play Aussie Rules football. Agatha! Agatha!'

'A couple of minor problems that even a technophobe like me can see with what you're trying there, Dingo love.'

'What's that, Maggs? Agatha … Agatha! Blimey, she's deafer than I am. Agatha! Play Aussie Rules. Strewth, Sharon said everyone she knows uses it. This is hopeless.'

'Well, I'm no expert, as I said, but I think the name's Alexa, for a start.'

'You sure, Maggs? Well, I'll give it a go: Alexa… ALEXA!'

'And you don't need to bellow unless you want the neighbours to watch the same thing you do.'

'Righto. Alexa,' he whispered. 'Alexa.'

'And your TV has to be connected to the internet. This one runs on steam.'

'Got it. Alexa!'

'And you have to have some sort of box – a speaker, or something – with Alexa installed. She doesn't pop in on her way back from the supermarket to change the channel for you.'

'We haven't got an Agatha?'

'No. She doesn't do the ironing or empty the bins, so I never got her installed.'

'Well, that was a waste of time. I'll switch the TV off and we can chat instead. Agatha. Switch off the TV.'

Maggie grabbed the remote, switched it off, and put it on the stool in front of them. 'Now, what was it you wanted to chat about?'

'Well, nothin' really.'

'Nothing?'

'Not much... other than... well...'

'About how horrendous it was to see a man on fire fall off a balcony? About who was behind the explosion in the flat? About why I left you at the hotel asleep while I went off to tackle the Head of the KGB? Or why Joshua and Bill left me – us – unsupported? Perhaps why Volkov was willing to put his head on the line to catch Stockley? Or even about what will happen to Stockley and Volkov now? You want to talk about that sort of thing?'

'Well, I was thinking more about what we are gonna have for tea, but since you mention it...'

'You have a right to know what we will have for tea, but while we wait for our enormous beef roast to go down, why don't I fill you in a bit more?'

They had, of course, talked about that crazy day a couple of weeks ago, but it had taken a while for Maggie to get the whole picture.

Yesterday evening, Dingo had been out playing pool with a few old boys in town who he had got to know. If he and Maggie were going to continue to spend half the year in Frampton, it was important that he had his own interests. Maggie had taken the opportunity to meet with Joshua for a full debrief.

It turned out that Joshua and Bill had been keeping an eye on her and Dingo for the whole time. Chauffeur Kim had been one of the contacts doing that job, but Maggie's great-grandson and son had been in the background, watching and waiting, hoping that she would lead them to Steinman so that they could step in and protect him.

Steinman's coming out of isolation hadn't been straightforward. Soon after the announcement and initial media interest, he had disappeared, squirrelled away – as they now knew – by Volkov who didn't trust the Secret Service any more than he trusted his own people. He did, however, as he declared to Maggie, trust her to make some sort of arrangements for Steinman, which was why he had Stockley intercept her and Dingo at the airport. What he didn't know was that someone in the Kremlin had it in for him – classic Kremlin power struggle. Stockley was working for that person – still unknown – as well as taking in work and a financial boost from the Iranians as a sideline.

'Don't get me wrong, Maggs – I love Joshua and Bill to bits, but weren't you pissed off they used you? You were put in danger. We both were.'

'It wouldn't be the first time I'd been thrown into the lion's den. It is – was – my job. They tried to contact me, to begin with, but when I didn't answer their calls, they decided to let it play out. They knew I wouldn't be able to resist getting involved. What I didn't like was putting you in danger, which was why I left you at the hotel in the end.'

'I gotta say that when I woke up, I was more worried than a wombat squeezin' one out and realising it's cube-shaped.'

Maggie ignored the metaphor which strictly only worked anyway if wombat's excrement wasn't cube-shaped, which it was. Another Dingo-ism, and she loved him for it.

'You looked so peaceful.'

'Knackered, more like.'

'Yes.' She squeezed his hand. 'I had to do the last bit on my own.'

He nodded. 'Yeah, I get it. Did you know it was Volkov who texted me about the meeting?'

Maggie nodded. 'I suspected so.'

'How did he get my number, by the way?'

'He's the head of the KGB.'

'Enough said. Did you know it was Steinman in the flat?'

'No. There was a lot I didn't know at that stage. That's why I went to meet Volkov. I was still dreadfully worried that Bill and Joshua might have been in the flat. I had no firm evidence for that, other than because I was involved, I thought they would be involved. I didn't know Steinman was there alone, and I didn't know Stockley arranged the explosion. Stockley had found out where Steinman was before we arrived at the embassy. The Kremlin, who wanted Steinman disposed of because of what he had done in the past, had presumably found out about Volkov's involvement and then decided he had to go too.'

'And you led them to Volkov.'

'Unintentionally. I knew someone was on my tail, but there wasn't a lot I could do about it. Fortunately, Joshua and Bill were on it.'

'You were on it too, Maggs. You're a demon with the knitting needle.'

'It's my superpower.'

'So, what will happen to Stockley now?'

'He'll be tried for espionage and conspiracy to murder. The police and Service will try to establish who arranged the explosion. It might have been one of the people they picked up at Tower Bridge.'

'And the people Stockley was working for?'

'That's more complicated. I doubt Stockley will talk. He'll be too scared of the consequences. Volkov certainly won't tell us; it's Kremlin business. I think he wanted to send a message out to whoever was behind this that he wasn't to be messed with, that he could outsmart them. They wouldn't have liked it, but he'll survive as Head of the KGB, at least for a bit longer.'

'I'd like to get that vision of Steinman on fire out of my head.'

Maggie turned and stroked his face. 'Me too. He was a good man.'

'Volkov obviously thought so. He risked a lot. So did you, my clever spy-wife.'

'And you, my funky backpacker.'

Dingo nudged her gently in the ribs. 'I prefer hunky outbacker, but I'll take that. Though I'm not planning to backpack anywhere at the moment, funkily or otherwise. I like it here.'

'I like it anywhere, as long as you're there with me.'

She put her arm through his and snuggled in close. They sat staring at the blank TV screen for a while.

She would have quite happily nodded off if she hadn't been startled by Dingo suddenly calling out: 'Agatha! Agatha! Make me a cheese sandwich for tea.'

Maggie sat up with a mock offended look on her face. 'I hope, Dingo Parfitt, that's not a clumsy attempt to suggest that I make you a cheese sandwich?'

Dingo wasn't great at looking contrite, so she had to smile at his half-hearted attempt. 'Course not, Maggs. I would never expect you to be a skivvy for me.'

She sat back with her arms folded. 'Good.'

Dingo pulled the stool closer in and grabbed the remote before stretching out on the sofa, his head on the armrest at the other end, his long legs dangled out over her. He threw the remote onto what bit of her lap wasn't covered by his legs, before placing his hands behind his head and easing it into the cushion he'd placed underneath.

'Though, wench, if you could find something on the telly I could nod off to, I'd be grateful.'

Maggie decided she had to be losing her touch. Missing a head that size with a remote from three feet away was a cardinal sin that no spy worth their salt should ever commit.

Maggie Matheson: Bonus Content

Maggie Matheson:

When Maggie Met Frankie

Maggie Matheson:

Going Loco in Lockdown

Maggie Matheson:

Mini-spy Special

Author's note

The following three even shorter and sweeter stories were written some time ago as Valentine's Day, Lockdown, and Christmas specials. This is the first time they have appeared in print.

Going Loco in Lockdown and *Mini-spy Special* can be read as standalone stories – Maggie being Maggie in two contrasting situations.

For the *When Maggie Met Frankie* story, readers who have not read the other 3 books in the Maggie Matheson Collection should know that Dingo Derek is Maggie's second husband. Maggie was married before to fellow spy (and father to Bill and Sharon) Frankie Matheson, now deceased. This is the story of how Maggie and Frankie met.

You may have noticed that the title is a parody of the Billy Crystal and Meg Ryan film *When Harry Met Sally*. For absolute clarity and to prevent possible litigation, I feel obliged to point out that no Harrys or Sallys were used, or harmed, during the making of this story.

Sit back with a nice cuppa and enjoy this Maggie bonus content.

Maggie Matheson: When Maggie Met Frankie

'Catch the 12:22 to Liverpool Street,' the briefing had said. 'Your liaison will be incognito. They will make contact with you.'

Maggie was happy enough with that. She had always enjoyed travelling on trains. It was her favourite mode of transport, by far. She settled herself down in a seat on the right-hand side which, in her opinion, provided the better views of the flat, but pleasantly rural, Essex countryside.

She had met her future husband, Frankie, on a train in 1953, on her way to work in a department store in the West End of London. 14th February 1953 – easy to remember. As the train pulled away from the station now, she could almost see Frankie catching her eye as he walked down the carriage before plonking himself right next to her, from where he set about wooing her with his charm. There had been enough wooing and enough charming to persuade her to go on a date, marry him eight months later... and, soon after that, join him as an agent in Her Majesty's Secret Service.

Back then, she had lived in Dagenham, in the East End, not that far from Theydon Bois, a much smarter area. Wanting to impress this mysterious, handsome man when he asked where she was from, she had lied

71

and said she was Theydon Bois, pronouncing the '*Bois*' part of name as the French might, '*bwar*'. Frankie's contagious laugh was what made her almost instantly fall in love with him.

'Blimey, Gal,' he had drawled. 'You're definitely not from there. It's pronounced Theydon 'Boys' not flamin' Theydon 'Bwaaaarrr'.

They were married in Walthamstow – his 'manor', as he called it – and had celebrated with a good old Eastend knees-up. Her parents, with pretensions of grandeur, might have argued he was from the 'wrong side of the tracks'. But, having died during the war, they were in no position to object either to Frankie's direct and bubbly personality, nor the location and informal style of wedding. Maggie's grandmother, who had taken over the parenting, had no such qualms for her granddaughter and had had a thoroughly lovely time at the reception. Maggie, with some guilt, said to Frankie that it was the after-effects of leading the conga down Walthamstow High Street at two o'clock in the morning on a chilly autumnal night that sounded the death knell for Nan, who died three weeks later. Frankie, of course, vehemently dismissed Maggie as being at fault, adding, tongue-in-cheek, that maybe they should process 'conga-style' at the funeral in tribute to Nan.

Maggie was so besotted with Frankie that she barely batted an eyelid when he told her that, not only did he want to spend the rest of his life with her but that he also wanted to recruit her into the spy ring he was setting up as part of his job in MI5. Up until that point, he had led her to believe he drove the number 8 bus for a living. Others might have seen his attempts to court her and their subsequent marriage as a recruitment ploy, just to get her involved with the Service. Maggie had read articles, only recently, about undercover policemen dating and sometimes marrying women purely so they could gather evidence for criminal investigations. Naturally, what happened to those women was horrendous, but such tactics did not apply to her and Frankie. She had always been secure in the knowledge that the relationship that they had was based totally on love and mutual respect. He had proved that to her over and over again in their marriage, both by his actions and his daily declarations of love.

He always found a way, even when they were apart, to tell her how he felt. It ranged from a simple regular phone call (day or night) to notes being left in strategic places with strict instructions to open them in a certain order so she could see his messages on each day that he or she was away. She did not know how he had managed to swing it but one message even came to her in code via official governmental communication lines. Typically, he had taken the subsequent rollicking from on high on the chin... and done the same thing the following year.

Her first ever Service case was with Frankie, and she was reminded of it now as the train passed the floodlights of Chelmsford City's football ground. It had ended up with a frantic car chase and eventual crash of the suspects' car just outside 'The Den', the home of Millwall F.C. A cold, damp evening and not the most exotic of circumstances for a case finale. But the previous three and half weeks spent pursuing the three Czech agents across Europe had been totally exotic for a Dagenham girl such as her. Frankie had whooped with delight when Maggie had fired the shot from out of their car window into the suspects' back near-side tyre. It had forced them off the road and into a car park barrier from where she and Frankie were in a position to secure their quarry.

She remembered Frankie giving her a wink before dragging the dazed agents out of the car onto the tarmac where he handcuffed them... much to the astonishment of the Millwall home fans who had begun pouring out of the stadium at the end of the match. Frankie's words of apology as they waited for the backup team to take the suspects away, had stuck with her:

'Sorry about the driving, Maggie Love, and sorry too about the dodgy location... No offence, mate,' he added to a passing disgruntled-looking home fan, 'but being a West Ham fan, I'd hoped to end up somewhere with a bit more class than this.'

Exciting times, with many more joint cases to follow, most of them undercover where Maggie developed an uncanny knack for spotting enemy agents in a crowd from a mile away. But it had not all been good. Far from it. She and Frankie had been forced to give up for adoption their firstborn, Peter, at a time when the world was a very dangerous place and their country needed good agents, working full time and committed to the cause.

'You're both spies,' they had been told by a cold heartless Civil Service mandarin, 'trained to a high level. Trained to avoid accidents. Your son was an accident. We don't do accidents here.'

It ranked as one of the darkest times of her life; that and losing Frankie to lung cancer nine years ago. Their daughter, Sharon, had come along much later than Peter, and by that time the Service's views and attitudes had changed. Even then, she had had to make sacrifices she now regretted; too many days, nights and weeks away from her daughter, reliant on neighbours and friends to help out when Frankie was also away. But she had poured all of her love, including that she had reserved for Peter, into her daughter.

Too much though, Maggs. You pushed her away to the other side of the world, all the way to Australia.

As the train pulled to a halt at Liverpool Street station, Maggie fought back a tear. Her life had been tainted by tragedy, some might say.

Some might say, but not Maggie. At the age of 81, she still had her health, her friends, her family, and, of course, memories of her first love, Frankie.

Now though, Maggs, she told herself as she spotted a young man in a smart suit approaching her carriage, *you have a job to do.*

And while she was at it, she'll give her new 'incognito' acquaintance a few tips: it might be Valentine's Day, but the red rose in the lapel screamed out '*spy*.'

Maggie Matheson: Going Loco in Lockdown

Maggie sighed as she put her iPad back down on the kitchen table. She missed Sharon, her husband Craig, and her grandchildren so much. But seeing them all walk around, talk, cook, swim in their pool, play games or sit around watching TV, just doing normal, everyday activities, was a bonus that she could not have imagined when Sharon first moved over to Australia. She wished she had used FaceTime with them years ago. Yes, they had always spoken on the phone, but seeing them too made all the difference.

Their video chats were a twice weekly occasion now, sometimes more. Maggie was quite prepared to talk at all hours and was always sad when it was finished; she had nothing much else to do these days, particularly in the current circumstances.

She hated to admit it but she had the 21st Century to thank for that.

Previously an active member of the **LGBT** community – **Luddite Grannies Banning Technology** – she had initially resisted calls to get an iPhone, iPad or anything resembling it. Now she was hardly off it.

She had finally gone over to the dark side and become a convert, an Apple follower to her core, but it had taken some doing. A pandemic, in fact.

Her great-grandson, Joshua, had tried to insist she use a tablet on her first mission back after a lengthy – and very mundane – period of retirement from the Secret Service. She had refused, having coped with communication in her much-preferred way, either in person or over a good old-fashioned immobile telephone. As she used to say to anyone who cared to listen (which was most of her friends because few of them were not of an age when they could move out of ear-shot fast enough):

'It's all the hoops they want you to jump through online, even to do something as straightforward as renewing a bus pass. If I was fit enough to jump through hoops, I wouldn't need the bloody bus pass in the first place.'

When Joshua had again attempted to use his powers of persuasion to convince her how much easier everyday activities would be with a computer, tablet or Smartphone, she had, there and then, written out a list – on a piece of paper, naturally – of things she did regularly, and showed it to him. She vowed that if they could continue to be done without swiping anything, she would stay true to her principles.

The list was as follows:

- Eating, sleeping and daily ablutions
- Shopping
- Going to the bookies to place the occasional bet

- Meeting my friends
- Coach trips
- Gin and tonic at the social club
- Going for a walk
- Spying
- Booking and going to appts to the dentist /chiropodist /optician /GP / hairdresser/ anyone else who stops my body falling apart /sex therapist (or so she told the hairdresser)

Then Lockdown happened. And nearly the entire list was taken away from her. What was left was not enough to keep her occupied, especially since most places in the last item – the mainstay of her social life these days – were closed. (Except the GP... and the sex therapist who was doing a roaring trade with everyone being stuck at home).

To start with, she had carried on working as normal; the world of espionage was hardly likely to take note of self-isolation guidelines. The bad guys were still there, although it had occurred to her that blending in with other people, a key skill for spies, might prove more difficult with no one around. She had visions of agents scuttling across the main squares of European cities in grey coats and sunglasses, desperately looking for objects such as waste bins to hide behind in an attempt to remain incognito.

Initially, lack of I.T. skills had not been a hindrance on her return to work after retirement, despite communication within the Service being largely digital. Joshua helped. He had hidden from his bosses that he printed everything out in size 16 Aerial font for Maggie to read. In Lockdown, though, it was a struggle to justify delivering brown envelopes by hand every week to computer-illiterate grannies as being an 'essential' journey, particularly if there was a quicker way to do it. Joshua had tried combining the delivery with taking other essential items, but when the cupboard started groaning under the weight of jelly babies and gin, it became more difficult. Consequently, she began to lose touch.

The other issue was the risk to her health. She had spent most of her career as a spy either tactically avoiding dangerous situations or, if that was not possible, confronting them and dealing with them head-on. She thought she could do the same in Lockdown. But was it absolutely essential that she carry on? Probably not. The Service would cope without her. So, it was, with some reluctance, that she had shut up shop, stayed in, and only gone out for more gin and jelly babies when critical (usually when the cupboard got down to half full).

It had nearly driven her mad. What she wouldn't have given to go back to the good old days of her life before she was coaxed back into the Service by Joshua to tackle, ironically, a criminal gang specialising in hacking cyber security. That mission and the ones that followed had given her a new lease of life, one she had hoped to continue living for a good while yet. That had been taken away, and more. Now, even sitting at her favourite restaurant, Sukuel's, and listening to Paula Larkin explain in detail how she got her net curtains so clean, seemed a luxurious proposition.

In the end, boredom – no, it was more than that – desperation for any human contact – had made her give in to technology. She had Wi-Fi installed. How, she had no idea. Joshua sorted it, 'remotely,' as he put it. And the next day, she came across what she thought was someone playing 'Knock Down Ginger' but was, in reality, a delivery man leaving her a parcel with an iPad and phone inside.

Her relief at finding there were no instructions, and therefore would not be able to use it, was tempered by the fact that there was a small note with a website address which told her she could set it up online. She had phoned Joshua on the landline.

'The new phone's arrived.'

'Good. Do you want me to text you to see if it's working?'

'You can try. I assume it needs to be on?'

'You joke? Have you charged it?'

'I'm tempted – with incitement to cause criminal damage for making me want to throw the bloody thing through the window.'

'What's wrong?'

'I'll tell you what's wrong. It says there are instructions to set it up online.'

'That's standard.'

'Yes, but there's a hole in my bucket.'

'What?'

'You know the song – There's a hole in my bucket. Look it up – online – if you don't know it. I would send you a like...'

'A link, not a like. Likes are...'

'Don't bother explaining. I'd send you a link if I knew how to. But I can't anyway because there's a hole in my bucket.'

There was a short gap while Maggie assumed Joshua was doing what she had suggested: looking the phrase up online. Then Joshua came back on.

'Ah, I see your problem. You can't go online to set it up because you need the phone to go online in the first place, and that is not set up yet. Just as in the song, your action is dependent on something you haven't got.'

'I've got a bucket, Joshua, which is useful for many more things than this sodding phone at the moment. It doesn't need the info-net...'

'Internet.'

'... to work nor does it have a hole, so I could fill it with water, for one thing. I could also shout into it and hope Sharon hears me in Australia. I could even write a note, put it into the bucket and hurl it towards the chemist in town to order my prescription. Labelled 'email', of course, because that's their preferred method of communication. Having to use email, by the way, is just what we all need when ordering life-saving drugs. Tapping out on a tiny screen using tiny buttons the names of multi-lettered drugs with complicated Latin words that change to other words when you write them is not easy.'

Joshua had asked her to be patient and said that he would again 'sort it'.

The following day two parcels arrived; one with a tablet in and one with a phone, both fully charged and set up ready to use. On both items, Joshua had left a post-it note with an arrow pointing to the home button saying, 'Press me'. Maggie had and, rather than shrinking or growing like Alice, she had started a journey into her own Wonderland, full of mysterious characters and traps.

That was two weeks ago. Now Maggie had worked out how to FaceTime (or *'FierceTime* as she initially called it because she was in such a state by the time she eventually started talking) Sharon and some of her friends. It had helped to be able to see and chat with people – considerably helped. She was in contact with the outside world again and was starting to feel normal. Technology had been her saviour.

She still looked forward to the day she would physically be with people. To walk down the street without people jumping into ditches to maintain social distance. To stand at the door to thank a delivery driver for a parcel without them screaming and running away. To be opposite Paula Larkin at Sukuel's and choose what she wanted from the Special's board while she talked about her net curtains. And, of course, to hug her son Bill, his family, Joshua, her friends, the milkman, the dishy lad who worked in the dry cleaners...

There were still demands and difficult times ahead, but there were positives. And there was one habit that she, and others, she imagined, had developed during Lockdown which she hoped would not change once it was all over That was how a face-to-face encounter was ended.

From now on she decided, whether virtually or in person, everyone should say 'Goodbye', peer at the person in confusion for twenty seconds, then press the other person's nose.

It might just catch on.

Maggie Matheson: Mini-spy Special

The Frampton-on-Sea Christmas Fashion Show was about to begin and the village hall was packed to the rafters, abuzz with excited voices. A mince pie and half a cup of warm mulled wine already banked safely in their stomachs on the way in, Maggie and Joshua negotiated the knees which blocked the path between them and two empty wooden chairs to one side of a splendid catwalk erected that morning.

'I don't know why you insisted on coming along, Joshua,' said Maggie, nodding and smiling at familiar faces as they squeezed past. 'I could have got here and back by myself.'

'It's already dark,' said Joshua. 'I'm not happy you hanging about afterwards for the bus and then walking up that long drive to your flat on your own.'

'And what do you think I do on the days you're not in Frampton? Sit around at home in the hope that a Hells Angels chapter is passing by with enough space on the back of a bike for one of them to give me a lift into town?'

'I'm assuming, from what appears at first sight to be a rather random reference, that someone from a Hells Angels chapter has actually given you a lift into town on the back of their bike?'

'Of course not! Those heady days when I clambered on and off the back of motorbikes are long gone. I'm too old for that sort of thing... They always put me in a sidecar.'

There was a pause in the conversation, something that was often needed when people spoke with Maggie while they attempted to work out whether what she had just said should be taken with a large pinch of salt or not. Joshua knew from past experiences that his great-grandmother was well seasoned, so the pause, on this occasion, was used for them both to negotiate a particularly difficult section of feet and bags.

'This is a sleepy town,' Maggie continued as they finally arrived at their destination. 'I know you and I operate within the field of espionage, but the chances of me being assassinated whilst on the number 22 bus are pretty low... unless you have information to the contrary?'

'Not at all. I was in the area and I just thought I could save you some hassle.'

'Well, thank you. I do appreciate it.' And she did. It was a crisp evening. A warm car was preferable to a draughty bus shelter for sure.

Maggie removed her coat, folded it up and sat on it. In her younger days as a spy, she had done many hours on stakeouts in freezing rooms with nothing to sit on at all except a hard floor. Quite why she was so sensitive these days, she had no idea. She had considerably more natural padding now than she did then.

'I hope you're going to enjoy this,' she said. 'There's one particular star of the show who always smashes it, as far as I'm concerned.'

As Joshua settled in beside her, she noticed he did what she always did, which was to take a few seconds to glance around, sussing out his surroundings. That habit was as ingrained in him as it was in her. Always on the lookout, always spying.

'Listen to that,' he said after a moment. 'The sound of natter. This is one big natter-fest.'

'Can't beat a good natter. Does us all the world of good.'

'Apart from me, are you the youngest here?'

'Maybe, although some of the models are in their seventies, I believe.'

At that moment, a scratchy version of Slade's 'Merry Christmas Everybody' struck up. It invoked an immediate response as a hundred pairs of arms rose and started swaying from side to side. Between the waves, there were glimpses of beaming festive faces while Noddy belted out the chorus.

It was not Maggie's favourite song, so she sat back and took the opportunity to look at the Christmas decorations that adorned the ceiling and walls. The vicar and her hoard of helpers had gone to a lot of trouble to deck the hall with not only boughs of holly but with every other conceivable plant that was still green at this time of year. It was attractive but, Maggie decided, was more 'Tarzan's' jungle' than 'Santa's grotto'. She preferred the things that reminded her of the Christmases she spent with her late husband, Frankie, which Maggie always ensured were crammed with every Christmas cliché imaginable. She sighed. Happy days.

The song finished and the hubbub resumed. Shaken out of her reverie, Maggie picked up her handbag from the floor and held it out in front of her, gripping the sides firmly.

'What are you doing?' Joshua asked.

'I'm making sure Maureen can see my new bag.'

'Who's Maureen?'

'You know Maureen.'

'How would I know Maureen?'

'You told me that the Service knows everything about everyone.'

'Well, I don't think I quite said that. I said it was similar to in your day in that we had a wide network of intelligence, but that super-fast fibre optics enabled systematic analysis of terra-bytes of data in nanoseconds, with resultant enhanced profiling and targeting.'

'And my response was?'

'You said, "Eh?" as I recall.'

'Ooh...' She patted Joshua's knee excitedly. 'The curtains just twitched. I bet that'll be Dawn having a sneaky peak. She's so nervous. I told her she shouldn't be. If you've got a good body, flaunt it. That's what I say. Flaunt it before you haunt it.'

'Flaunt it before you haunt it?'

'Show it off before you kick the bucket. I thought you kids were into patois?'

'Hmm, I've got a feeling you just made that up.'

Maggie raised an eyebrow then lifted her bag higher up so that it rested in front of her chin. She peered over the top of it, her eyes sweeping across the rows in front until, eventually, she spotted a lady turning round to have a chat with someone behind. She nodded and smiled at her, giving the bag a subtle waggle, much in the way that holding the F.A. cup aloft at Wembley might be given a subtle waggle.

'Is that Maureen?' asked Joshua.

'Yes.'

'Explain to me exactly why you're showing her your bag?'

'I'm spreading the love. She'll be happy because I've got a new bag. Look, she's smiling and, oh, waving too. She definitely likes it.' Maggie gave a thumbs-up, pointed at it and said: 'I just got it from that new shop in the High Street, twenty per cent off in their pre-Christmas sale, made of faux leather but good quality. Lovely range of colours.' It drew a confused look.

'She can't hear you. You mouthed the whole thing.'

'Well, I don't want everyone hearing my business!'

'But you just said...'

'Look, here we go.' Maggie sat forward as a woman, dressed in a blue-pink tartan skirt, white blouse and matching tartan jacket, appeared from behind the curtain to the sound of jingling sleigh bells.

'It's about to start. That's Tania. You're going to love Tania.'

'Why, is she good?'

'Not at all. Her brother-in-law provides the clothes and she insists on presenting the fashion show. She's, um... unique. But we all love her. You'll see what I mean in a minute. And the theme, I see, is tartan... again! I hope they'll finish with Dougal playing his bagpipes.'

'Dougal?'

'His real name is Clive. Can't play the bagpipes that well, has a perpetual cold.'

'Then why...'

'Commitment and effort that's the main thing, isn't it?'

'Well, no. Lots of wind and the ability to play the bagpipes I would have thought might have been the bare minimum.'

'It will add a little something to what you're about to see, I'm sure.'

There was a shriek of, 'Helloooo, everyone!' and then Tania launched into, not so much of a patter, more of a splatter, as she attempted to disperse superlatives to all corners of the hall. 'Welcome to the fantastic, formidable fl... um...,' at this point, she glanced down at the card she held in her hand before continuing, 'fl... no... festive, frightening... that's not right... what does that say?' She stopped and reached for her reading glasses, strung around her neck. 'Let me see... Is that fractious... No, that can't be right.' She took off her glasses and used them to zoom in and out towards the card. 'Oh, blessed things. Sorry about this.' She turned around and called out, 'Joan... Joan...'

From behind the curtain, the crinkled face of a woman Maggie did not recognise appeared, so low down that it looked like she was sitting on a chair. The face was followed by the rest of Joan, one of the tiniest women Maggie had ever seen, dressed in exactly the same outfit as Tania. At an impossibly slow pace, she walked out to join the hostess. Keen to maintain her stage presence, Tania held her ground and waited, offering an apologetic smile to the audience before bending down and showing Joan the card. 'What does this word say, Joan?'

'Hang on, I'll get my glasses.' With that Joan did an about-face and shuffled off just as slowly, presumably to find her glasses. In the meantime, Tania picked a point at the back of the hall to stare at with a fixed smile as if it was all perfectly natural and planned.

'Why doesn't Tania just carry on?' whispered Joshua.

'She's very meticulous is Tania. Likes to get things right.'

'But nothing's happening.'

'I know! Isn't it brilliant! Tania's always entertaining.'

The audience sat, for the first time that evening, in silence waiting for Joan to re-emerge. This time, when she did, it seemed to Maggie that her face was even lower down the curtain, but at least she had reading glasses on. The tortuously slow journey out began again until she reached centre stage, where Tania handed her the card and pointed to the word. Joan looked at it and then beckoned her to bend down so she could whisper in her ear. There was an obvious light bulb moment for Tania, but she waited for Joan to walk off again before exclaiming, 'formidable, festive... Frampton... I should have known that word, Frampton. I can see the capital letter now. Yes, welcome to the fabulous, formidable...,' a quick check with the glasses again, '... festive Frampton fashion show!' She held her arms out, the cue for the audience to burst into rapturous applause.

'Is Tania always like this?'

'There's always a twist or two where Tania's concerned.'

The rest of the card must have been more legible as Tania gave a summary of the proceedings with no more help from Joan. This made it no less entertaining. Tania's voice was mainly very proper, but only to the extent that it sounded like someone doing an impression of someone acting a scene from Pride and Prejudice. Maggie had met Tania several times and knew her background and real voice. Brought up in Manchester, she was less, 'Good morning, Mr Darcy!' and more 'Hiya, Luv.' As she thanked the models in advance and the audience for their support for the event, her voice flip-flopped from Hyacinth Bouquet to Vera Duckworth.

But this was only the prelude to the main event as Tania finally introduced the first model: 'And now, fresh from doing a jig in the Highlands of bonny Scotland, I present to you: Daphne!'

With 'I'm on My Way' by the Proclaimers playing in the background, the curtains swept back to reveal the side view of a woman slightly hunched over, fiddling with a belt. She looked up, slightly surprised when the crowd welcomed her with a round of applause.

'That's not Daphne,' whispered Maggie. 'It's Glenda.'

'Oh. Will that be a problem?'

'I'm sure no one will mind too much, least of all Glenda. She's used to Tania.'

Belt adjusted to her satisfaction, Glenda smiled as she prepared to walk out onto the catwalk which lit up with twinkling blue and white lights on either side. Tania moved to the side of the stage to allow Glenda the freedom she needed and started her commentary: 'Daphne is wearing a chiffon blouse from the Edinburgh-based Dante summer collection. The pleated knee-length skirt with pink braiding complements her pink sandals, from the same collection, and is ideal for those warm Scottish summer evenings we all know and love.'

At the end of the catwalk, Glenda, who in her now firmly belted trousers, woollen green and red cardigan, black boots and thick winter coat was busy not being Daphne on a warm summer's evening, attempted an ambitious manoeuvre which nearly worked. Flicking her red scarf back over her right shoulder, she turned 180 degrees, took a step towards the home run-in and stumbled forward. There was a collective intake of breath as, teetering sideways, she diced with the catwalk's edge. Festive goodwill won the day, however, as the audience willed her to stay on her feet, and Glenda regained her balance and composure. Tania, busily pointing out the benefits of the light but resilient fabric of the skirt which was suitable both on a cool wash and at higher temperatures, seemed oblivious to Glenda's predicament.

As Glenda disappeared behind the curtain, the first line of the Skye Boat Song cut in, the cue for the next model – Daphne, judging by the outfit she was wearing, Meryl according to Tania – to set off. The fact that her most notable fashion accessory was a crutch only added to the warm atmosphere generated by everyone there.

'She's done well,' said Maggie. 'Her hip replacement was only two months ago. You have to admire her tenacity.'

The Skye Boat Song nearly drowned out Tania's attempts to describe the wrong clothes, but she raised her voice and ploughed on regardless. The evening continued with many slick displays from models – all of them having the time of their lives – and Tania finally in sync with the clothes being shown. The latter, Maggie found a tad disappointing, and she had hoped that Joan might make another appearance. They would have made a good double act, she decided.

Clive and his bagpipes brought the evening near to its climax with what Maggie later found out was the 'Flower of Scotland'. At points in the rendition, it was hard to tell whether it was Clive or his bagpipes that were making the honking and wheezing sounds that filled the hall. The grand finale with twenty models on stage standing all along the catwalk took a while to set up, particularly since Tania insisted on adjusting each of their positions to her exacting standards, but there was a standing ovation at the end of it.

'That was superb,' said Joshua as they filed past the Christmas tree towards the exit. 'I loved every minute of it.'

'I'm glad. Thanks for coming with me.' Maggie paused before asking, 'Did you get everything you needed?'

'What do you mean?'

'Did you get all the information you needed?'

'Information?'

'I may be eighty-one,' said Maggie, 'but I wasn't born yesterday.'

'That sounds like one of your Maggie-isms.'

'Well?'

Joshua coughed; a rather embarrassed sound which told Maggie she was on the right path. She waited, anticipating he would continue.

'Yes, if you must know, I did get what I needed... what we needed. How did you know we were after someone?'

'Joshua, I'm a spy, remember? Trained to notice things. So, is it a Russian, or an agent from one of the Middle Eastern countries?'

'Neither. But I'm afraid that's all you'll get from me.'

The smell of snow in the chilly air as they came out and the distant sounds of carols being sung gave the occasion the injection of atmosphere Maggie loved. But her mind was on other things too as she noticed an unmarked white van parked by the side of the hall. She ignored Joshua's pleas and made straight for it, squeezing down the side and past the two open doors at the back. Coming out of the side door of the hall, squirming and cursing, was a figure she immediately recognised.

Despite her diminutive size and age, she was making it difficult for the two considerably larger men on either side of her who were stooping as they frogmarched her towards the van. In the end, the men stood upright and lifted her off the ground, leaving her legs kicking out in all directions until they got her into the back. The men joined her inside and the doors were slammed shut before the van pulled out onto the main Frampton seafront road. Maggie could still hear the woman's voice as it rounded the corner.

She turned to Joshua. 'Joan! I should have guessed. Well, well. I hope she was worth the effort.'

'Oh, she was definitely worth the effort. Shall we...?'

'Oh, don't worry. Looks like I've got a lift back.' Joshua turned round at the sound of a motorbike engine revving.

'Okay, well, I'll see you Christmas Day. Until then, remember that what you've just seen is dealt with on a need-to-know basis.' Joshua mimicked zipping his mouth up, and made to turn away.

Maggie grabbed his arm and pulled him back. 'I'll make one more comment only and then say no more.'

'I doubt that, but go on.'

'This Joan...'

'Yes?'

'Isn't she a bit old to be a spy?'

Other Maggie books

If you enjoyed this collection of short stories about Maggie Matheson, you may well enjoy the longer novel format below.

All of them are available on Amazon.

Maggie Matheson: The Senior Spy

Maggie Matheson: Down Undercover

Maggie Matheson: Last Orders

About the Author

Ian lives in Colchester in the UK and is the only right-handed former teacher, former customs officer, current author, and current Toblerone-lover to support Colchester United FC, as far as he knows.

Unlike Maggie, he is not a spy, current or former.

Definitely not... or is he?

No.

Reviews and Social Media

Thank you for reading this book. Ian would love to know what you think it, so why not leave a review on Amazon or Goodreads?

Or contact Ian on the social media links below:

Website www.ianhornett.com

Facebook
@ianmichaelhornett

Instagram
@ianhornett

Printed in Dunstable, United Kingdom